This igloo book belongs to:

....

igloobooks

Published in 2020
First published in the UK by Igloo Books Ltd
An imprint of Igloo Books Ltd
Cottage Farm, NN6 0BJ, UK
Owned by Bonnier Books
Sveavägen 56, Stockholm, Sweden
www.igloobooks.com

1220 001
2 4 6 8 10 9 7 5 3 1
ISBN 978-1-83903-315-5

Written by Stephanie Moss
Illustrated by Benedetta Capriotti

Designed by Bethany Dowling
Edited by Daisy Edwards

Printed and manufactured in China.

The Stars Have All GONE OUT

igloobooks

The stars have all gone out.
Why have they gone away?
I'm sure that they were out there
when I looked just yesterday.

I counted every one of them before I went to bed.

You promised they'd **shine** down on me, but now it's **dark** instead.

"Don't worry, Little Bear. Everything will be alright,"

says Mummy when she tucks me in and kisses me goodnight.

I dive under the covers till I've come up with a plan.
The stars make me feel safe at night. I'll fix them if I can!

Soon I'm floating up, up
on a big, bright red balloon.
I fly through outer space
until I've landed on the Moon.

I look out of my telescope, then sit and watch for hours.

I still can't see a single star among the comet showers.

"Do you know where the stars have gone?" I ask a passerby.

"The fairies over there can help!" is his friendly reply.

I join the twinkle fairies,
with their huge star-fishing net,
to scoop up all the little stars
that haven't turned on yet.

But some stars can be naughty
and they like to *WHOOSH* away!

"Please don't go!" I call to them.

"We need your help," I say.

When I catch them up, I help the friendly stars to see,
that if they all come back, they'll comfort little bears like me.

"Let's paint you rainbow colours,"
I say. "Pink, purple and blue!
Then the whole wide galaxy will
see you shining, too."

Next we climb up ladders
that are 15 houses high.
We sing the sweetest lullabies
and place stars in the sky.

When our work is done, the night sky looks as good as new.

"Thank you," say the fairies, "and it's all because of you!"

My friends save me a star and whisper, "This one's yours to keep.
Take it back to bed with you to help you fall asleep."

My red balloon goes **POP** and very soon I'm floating home.

My star is brightly shining, so I'll never feel alone.

I snuggle up in bed,

as Mummy looks around the door.

I point towards the sky and say,

"It's not dark any more!"

Mummy hugs me tightly and says, "Little Bear, well done!
Your outer-space adventure must have been a lot of fun.

But if you're feeling worried, you don't have to go that far.

You don't need to go to space and paint all of the stars."

"Sometimes when it's cloudy or the sun has just gone down,
or lights are shining brightly from a very busy town...

... the stars aren't quite as shiny as we'd like them all to be,

but you can always have a cuddle specially from me!"